Zoo Day

BY *Anne Rockwell*
ILLUSTRATED BY *Lizzy Rockwell*

ALADDIN • New York • London • Toronto • Sydney • New Delhi

for Sullivan

On a sunny Saturday, I go to the zoo with my mother, father, and sister, Lucy.

It's my very first time there.

Lucy's, too.

My father buys a ticket for each of us, and a bag of popcorn to share.

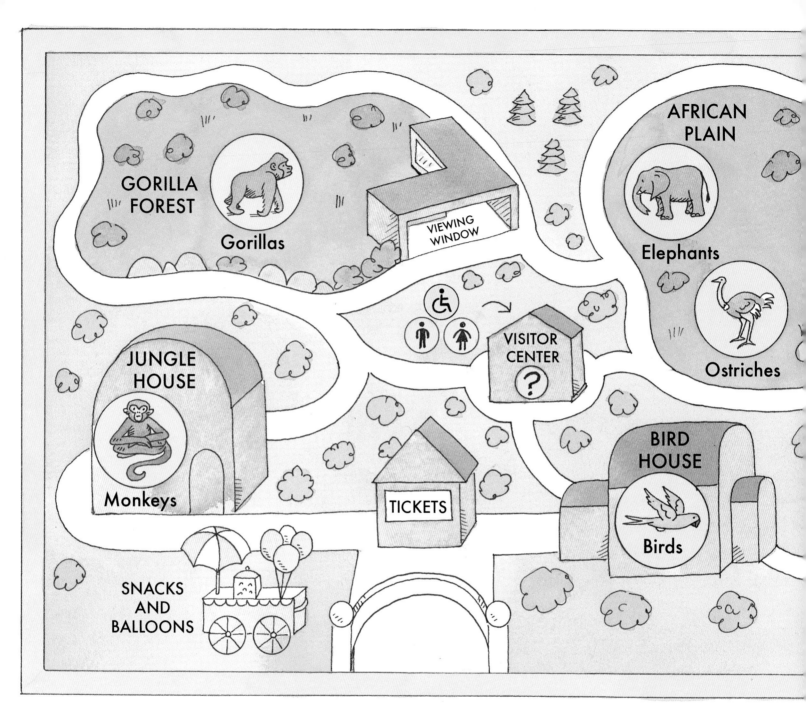

While we look at the map, I can hear roars and howls,
chitter-chatter and songs, cries and squawks.

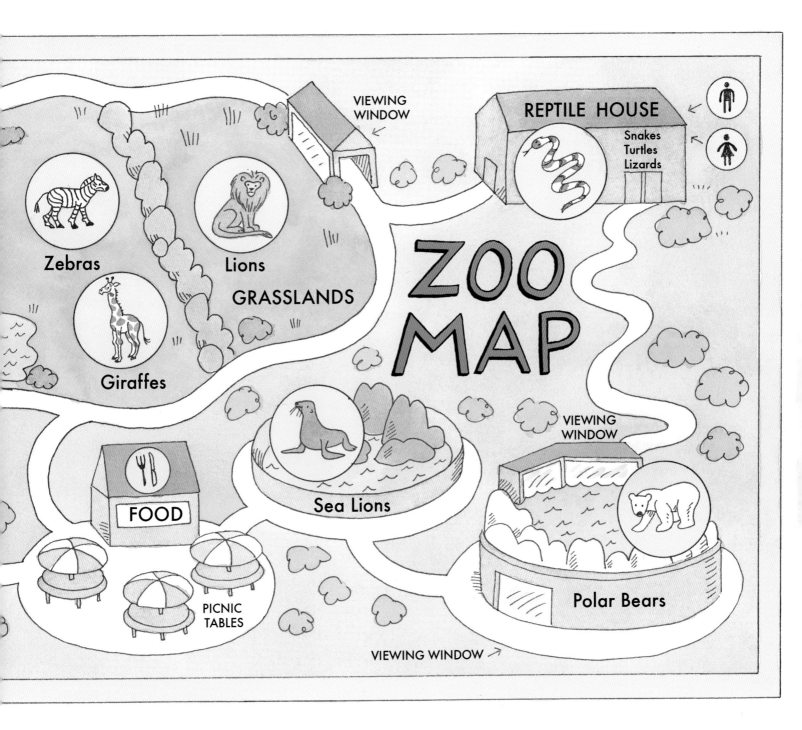

I hold my father's hand tightly because the roars make me a little nervous.

First we go into the Jungle House
to say hello to the monkeys.

Next we visit the Gorilla Forest.

The big gorilla comes right up to the window.

She stares at me so hard, I feel like I'm in the zoo and she's the visitor.

At the African Plain we find a mother elephant and her baby.

The baby elephant sticks very close to its mother.

There are funny-looking ostriches, zebras, and giraffes munching leaves off the trees.

Inside the Grasslands building I can see the big lion with the yellow mane.

He looks sleepy and quiet, but all of a sudden he opens his mouth and *roarrrrrrs*.

"It must be his naptime," Lucy says. "I bet he's telling us to shush and let him sleep."

Then we visit the Reptile House.

We see a giant boa constrictor and a tiny coral snake.

The coral snake is very pretty but very poisonous.

There is a turtle swimming in a tank.

Coral
Snake

Painted
Turtle

We walk along the shady path
to where the polar bears live.

Lucy loves polar bears.

She has a big stuffed animal polar bear at home and it's her favorite toy.

REPTILES

POLAR BEARS

We love to watch the polar bears in their underwater dance.

We could watch them all day.

But my father says, "It's almost time. Let's go."

We hurry over to the big pond where the sea lions live.

They're climbing on rocks and sliding off, and they're barking and splashing and grunting.

Lucy laughs. "They sound just like Roxy."

Roxy is our pet beagle.

I laugh, too.

When the zookeeper comes to feed them,
the sea lions gather around, barking even louder.

She throws a shiny fish up in the air.

A sea lion catches it and slaps his flipper on the rock.

Another catches a fish and dives underwater.

"Now they're making me hungry," I tell my mom.

"Me too," she says.

We sit at a picnic table and unpack our lunch.

Just as soon as we finish, I hear a whistling sound.

What's that? I wonder.

We follow the sound to the Bird House.

But the birds aren't in cages!

They are flying all over and all around us,
but they don't fly out the door.

Lucy and I hold up small cups of nectar.

A parrot stands on my shoulder and takes a sip.

I wish I could bring him home.

But we can't bring home any of the animals we've seen.

Just the same, Dad buys us two balloons.

One with a polar bear for Lucy, and one with a parrot for me to remember our day at the zoo.

ALADDIN

An imprint of Simon & Schuster Children's Publishing Division

1230 Avenue of the Americas, New York, NY 10020

First Aladdin hardcover edition January 2017

Text copyright © 2017 by Anne Rockwell

Illustrations copyright © 2017 by Lizzy Rockwell

All rights reserved, including the right of reproduction in whole or in part in any form.

ALADDIN is a trademark of Simon & Schuster, Inc., and related logo is a registered trademark of Simon & Schuster, Inc.

For information about special discounts for bulk purchases, please contact Simon & Schuster Special Sales at 1-866-506-1949 or business@simonandschuster.com.

The Simon & Schuster Speakers Bureau can bring authors to your live event. For more information or to book an event contact the Simon & Schuster Speakers Bureau at 1-866-248-3049 or visit our website at www.simonspeakers.com.

Designed by Jessica Handelman

The illustrations for this book were rendered in watercolor.

The text of this book was set in Caslon.

Manufactured in China 0721 SCP

10 9 8 7 6 5 4 3

Library of Congress Control Number 2016932615

ISBN 978-1-4814-2734-0 (hc)

ISBN 978-1-4814-2736-4 (eBook)